P9-DNN-269

THE SNOW QUEEN

HANS CHRISTIAN ANDERSEN

THE
SNOW QUEEN

With illustrations by
MARCIA BROWN

CHARLES SCRIBNER'S SONS · NEW YORK

To my Mother

Copyright © 1972 Marcia Brown

Translation by R. P. Keigwin used by permission
of Flensted Publishers, Odense, Denmark

This book published simultaneously in
the United States of America and in Canada—
Copyright under the Berne Convention

All rights reserved. No part of this book
may be reproduced in any form without
the permission of Charles Scribner's Sons.

A–8.72 [M2]

Printed in the United States of America

Library of Congress Catalog Card Number 72–168499
SBN 684–12611–7

T 2584

VENTURA COUNTY SCHOOLS LIBRARY
VENTURA, CALIFORNIA

The Snow Queen

170304

PART ONE

*The looking glass
and the broken bits*

NOW look out! We're going to begin. When we've come to the end of this part, we shall know more than we do now; for it has to do with a wicked imp—one of the very wickedest—Old Nick. One day he was in excellent spirits because he had made a looking glass which had this about it—that everything good and beautiful that was reflected in it shrank up into almost nothing, whereas everything useless and ugly stood out worse than ever. In this glass the loveliest scenery looked like boiled spinach, and even the nicest people became nasty or stood on their heads and had no stomachs. Faces were so twisted that you couldn't recognize them, and if you happened to have one freckle you could be sure that it would spread all over nose and mouth. That was huge fun, according to Old Nick. Suppose a person had some kind, good thought, a horrible leer was reflected in the looking glass, which made Nick roar with laughter at his clever invention. Everyone who went to the imp-school—for he kept a school for imps—went about saying there had been a miracle: now for the first time (they declared) one could see what people and things really looked like. They ran about all over the place with the looking glass, till at last there wasn't a country or a person that hadn't been changed for the worse in this way.

And now they decided to fly up to heaven and make fun of the angels and of God Himself. The higher they flew with the looking glass, the more horribly it leered—they could scarcely hold on to it. Up and up they went, nearer and nearer to God and the angels. All at once the glass quivered so terribly from its grimace that it flew out of their hands and went crashing down to earth, where it burst into a hundred million billion pieces, and even more than that; in fact, it now did much worse damage than before. You see, some pieces were hardly bigger than a grain of sand; and these flew round the whole wide world, and whenever they got into people's eyes they stuck there, and a person saw everything wrong or saw only the worst side of a thing, for every

little glass splinter had kept the same powers as the whole looking glass. Some people even got a little bit of glass in their hearts, and that was too terrible; the heart became just like a lump of ice. A few fragments were so big that they got used as windowpanes, but it was better not to see your friends through windows of that sort. Other pieces were fitted into spectacles, and when people put on their glasses in order to see properly and fairly, then things didn't go at all well; and the devil laughed till he split—he was simply tickled to death.

But outside there were still little bits of glass whirling about in the air. Just listen to what happened.

PART TWO

A little boy
and a little girl

IN the great city—where there are so many houses and people that there isn't room for everyone to have a little garden of his own, so most of them have to be content with flowers in flowerpots—there lived two poor children who *did* have a garden a bit larger than a flowerpot. They weren't brother and sister, but they were just as fond of each other as if they had been. Their parents were next-door neighbors, living in attics; at the point where their roofs were almost touching and the gutter ran along between the eaves, each house had a window facing the other. You had only to step over the gutter to cross from window to window.

The parents of the two children each had a big wooden box outside, and in this grew pot-herbs, which they used, and a little rose tree; there was one in each box, and they grew beautifully. Then the parents thought of placing the boxes across the gutter in such a way that they nearly reached from one window to the other and looked exactly like two banks of flowers. The sweet pea tendrils hung down over the boxes; the rose trees put out long branches, twining round the windows and leaning toward each other; it was almost a triumphal arch of greenery and flowers. As the boxes were very high and the two children knew that they mustn't crawl up on them, they often got leave to climb out to each other and, sitting on their little stools under the roses, had wonderful games there together.

In winter, of course, that sort of fun came to an end. The windowpanes were often frosted right over; but then they warmed up pennies on the stove, placed the heated coin on the frozen pane, and in this way made a splendid peephole, as round as could be. Behind, there peeped a gentle, loving eye, one from each window. It was the little boy and the little girl; his name was Kay, hers was Gerda. In summer they could reach each other with a single jump; in winter they must go down a lot of stairs, then up a lot of stairs, while outside the snow would be steadily falling.

"Those are the white bees swarming," said the old grandmother.

"Have they got a queen as well?" asked the little boy, for he knew that real bees have a sort of queen.

"Yes, they have," said the grandmother. "She flies just where the swarm is thickest, and she's the biggest of them all. She never lies still on the ground; she flies up again into the black cloud. On many a winter night she flies through the streets of the town and peeps in at the windows, and then they freeze into curious patterns, just like flowers."

"Yes, I've seen that!" cried both children at once, and so they knew it was true.

"Can the Snow Queen come in here?" asked the little girl.

"Just let her have a go," said the boy; "I'll put her on the hot stove, and she'll melt."

But the grandmother smoothed his hair and told them some other stories.

In the evening, when little Kay was home again and half-undressed, he crawled up on the chairs by the window and peeped out through the little hole. A few snowflakes were falling outside, and one of these, the biggest of them all, remained lying on the edge of one of the flower boxes. The snowflake grew larger and larger, till at last it became the figure of a woman dressed in the most delicate white gauze, which was made up of millions of tiny star-shaped flakes. She was pretty and distinguished-looking, but a figure of ice,

18

glaring glittering ice. Yet she was alive; her eyes stared like two bright stars, but there was no peace or quiet in them. She nodded towards the window and beckoned with her hand. The little boy grew frightened and jumped down from the chair; and at that moment a large bird seemed to fly past the window.

Next day there was a clear frost, and this was followed by a thaw; after that came the spring. The sun shone, bits of green peeped out, the swallows built their nests, the windows were thrown open, and once more the two little children sat in their little garden high up by the gutter at the very top of the house.

The roses were especially fine that summer. The little girl had learnt a hymn that had a bit about roses in it, and these roses made her think of her own. She sang it to the little boy, and he joined in:

> The valley glows with many a rose,
> and there we meet the Sacred Child.

And the two children took each other's hands and kissed the roses; they looked up at God's bright sunshine and spoke to it as if the Holy Child were there. What beautiful summer days those were! How wonderful it was to be out beside the fresh rose trees, which never seemed to want to stop blooming!

Kay and Gerda sat looking at the picture book of birds and animals, when suddenly, just as five o'clock was striking from the tall church tower, Kay called out, "Ow! something's pricked me in the heart. Ow! and now I've got something in my eye."

The little girl put her arm round his neck; he blinked his eyes. No, there was nothing to be seen.

"I expect it's gone," he said. But it hadn't gone. It just happened to be one of those glass splinters that flew from the looking glass—the imp glass—you remember, don't you, that

20

horrid glass which made everything great and good that was reflected in it seem small and ugly, while what was evil and wicked stood out sharply and every flaw showed up at once. Sure enough, poor Kay had received a piece right in his heart, which would presently turn into a lump of ice. For the moment the piece of glass had stopped hurting, but it was still there.

"Gerda, why are you crying?" he asked. "It makes you look so ugly. There's nothing whatever the matter with me. Ugh!" he cried suddenly, "that rose has got a worm in it, and look how crooked that one's growing. They're rotten roses, when you come to think of it—just like the boxes they're growing in." And he kicked the box hard and broke off the two roses.

"Kay, what are you doing?" exclaimed the little girl; and when he saw how upset she was, he broke off another rose and ran in at his window away from dear little Gerda.

Next time she got out the picture book, he said the book was babyish; and if their grandmother told them stories, he always chipped in with an "Ah, but—." He would even, if he got the chance, go behind her, put on some spectacles and talk just like her. It was a perfect imitation and made people laugh. After a while he could mimic the voice and the walk of every single person in the street. Kay knew how to take off all their awkward peculiarities, so that people said, "That boy certainly has a remarkable head on him." But no, it was the bit of glass in his eye, the bit of glass in his heart, that made him tease even little Gerda, who loved him from the bottom of her heart.

The games he played now were quite different from the old ones; they were quite brainy. One winter's day, as the snowflakes were drifting down, he picked up a big burning-glass and, holding out the flap of his blue coat, he let the snowflakes fall on it.

"Take a peep through this glass, Gerda," he said; and every snowflake became much larger and looked like a splendid flower or a ten-pointed star. It was a wonderful sight.

"Do you see how cunning that is?" said Kay. "These are much more interesting than real flowers. And there isn't

a single flaw in them; they are perfect in every way, as long as they don't melt."

A little later Kay arrived with big gloves on and his toboggan on his back. He shouted into Gerda's ears that he had been told he might go tobogganing in the main Square where the others were playing, and away he went.

Over in the Square the boldest boys often tied their toboggans onto the farmer's cart and in that way went with it a good distance. It was grand sport. In the midst of the fun a large sledge drove up, all painted dead white. In it sat a figure, muffled in a white fur coat and wearing a white fur cap. The sledge drove twice round the Square, and in a twinkling Kay managed to fasten his toboggan behind it so that it pulled him along. Faster and faster they went, straight into the next street. The driver of the sledge, with a turn of the head, gave Kay a friendly nod just as though they knew each other; and each time that Kay thought of loosening his little toboggan, the person nodded again, and so Kay stayed where he was, and they drove straight out of the town gate. Now the snow began to fall so thickly that the boy couldn't see his hand in front of his face as he rushed along. He quickly let loose the rope so as to get away from the big sledge. But that was no use; his little toboggan still clung to it, and they scudded along like the wind. He yelled at the top of his voice, but no one heard him; and the snow whirled down, and the sledge flew on. Now and then it did a jump, as though they

were crossing ditches and hedges. Kay was absolutely terrified; he tried to say the Lord's Prayer, but all he could remember was the multiplication table.

The snowflakes got bigger and bigger, till at last they looked like great white chickens. All at once they sprang aside, the big sledge stopped, and the driver stood up. Coat and cap were pure snow; it was a woman, tall and straight, white and glittering. It was the Snow Queen.

"We've covered the ground well," she said. "But do you feel cold? Creep into my bearskin." And she put him beside her in the sledge and wrapped the furs round him; it was like sinking into a snowdrift.

"Are you still cold?" she asked, and then she kissed his forehead. Uh! Her kiss was colder than ice, it went right to his heart, which was anyhow nearly a lump of ice already. He felt as if he were dying—but only for a moment. After that all was well, and he didn't notice the cold any more.

"My sledge! Don't forget my little sledge!" That was the first thing he thought of, and it was fastened to one of the white chickens, which came flying along behind them with the toboggan on its back. The Snow Queen kissed Kay once more, and after that he had quite forgotten little Gerda and Grannie and all the others at home.

"You mustn't have any more kisses," said the Snow Queen, "or else I shall kiss you to death."

Kay looked at her. She was very beautiful; he couldn't imagine a more intelligent, lovelier face. She no longer seemed to be just a figure of ice, as she did that time she sat outside the window and beckoned to him. In his eyes she was perfect. He didn't feel a bit afraid, but described to her how he could do mental arithmetic, even with fractions, and that he knew the number of square miles there were to the different countries and "what's the population?" And she kept smiling back at him, so that he began to think that perhaps what he knew was hardly enough. And he looked up into the great spaces of the sky, and she flew along with him, high up on the black cloud; and the wind roared and whistled—it reminded one of the old folksongs. They flew over woods and lakes, over sea and land; below them the icy blast whistled, the wolves howled, the snow sparkled as the black crows flew screaming across it; but high above everything shone the great silver moon. Kay gazed up at it through the long, long winter night; by day he slept at the Snow Queen's feet.

PART THREE

*The flower garden
of the old woman
who could do magic*

BUT how was little Gerda getting on, when Kay didn't come back? Wherever had he got to? No one knew, no one could give any news of him. The boys simply described how they had seen him tie his toboggan to a fine great sledge which drove down the street and out by the town gate. Nobody knew where he was. There was great grief, and little Gerda cried her heart out. Then people said he was dead, that he had fallen into the river which ran close to the town. What a long, gloomy winter it was!

And now the spring arrived with warmer sunshine.

"Kay's dead and gone," said little Gerda.

"I don't believe it," said the sunshine.

"He's dead and gone," she said to the swallows.

"I don't believe it," was the answer; and in the end little Gerda didn't believe it either.

"I'll put on my new red shoes," she said one morning. "The ones Kay has never seen, and I'll then go down to the river and question it."

It was early morning when she kissed her sleeping Grannie, put on the red shoes and walked all by herself out of the town gate down to the river.

"Is it true that you've taken my little playmate? I'll give you my red shoes, if you'll give him back to me."

And the waves seemed to nod back at her curiously. Then she took off her red shoes, the dearest possession she had, and threw them both out into the river; but they fell close in to the bank, and the little waves brought them straight back to her. It was just as though the river didn't like to rob her of her dearest possession because anyhow it hadn't taken little Kay. But now Gerda felt that perhaps she hadn't thrown the shoes far enough out; so she climbed into a boat that lay among the rushes and went right along to the far end of it and threw the shoes overboard. But the boat had not been made fast, and at the movement she gave it, it drifted from the bank. She noticed this and made haste to escape, but before she could get back the boat was a couple of yards from the shore, and now it gathered speed as it glided away.

At this Gerda grew very frightened and began to cry, but nobody heard her except the sparrows, and they couldn't carry her ashore, but they flew along the bank, as if to comfort her with their chirping, "Here we are, here we are!" The boat drifted with the stream, while little Gerda sat quite still in her stocking feet. Her red shoes were floating behind, but they couldn't catch the boat, which had more way on.

It was very pretty on both banks: old trees, lovely flowers, and grassy slopes with sheep and cows, but not a person in sight.

"Perhaps the river will carry me to little Kay," thought Gerda, and that raised her spirits. She stood up and gazed for hours at the delightful green banks. Eventually she came to a large cherry orchard, where there was a little house with curious red and blue windows, also a thatched roof and two wooden soldiers outside presenting arms to all who sailed past.

Gerda called out to them, thinking they were alive, but of course they didn't answer. She came quite close to them, as the river drove the boat straight into the bank.

Gerda called out still louder, and that brought out of the house an old, old woman leaning on a crutch-handled stick; she was wearing a large sun hat, which was painted over with most beautiful flowers.

32

"You poor child!" said the old woman. "How ever did you come to be driven onto this great rolling river, far out into the wide world?" Then the old woman went right into the water and, hooking the boat with her stick, drew it in to the bank and lifted little Gerda out. Gerda was glad to be on dry land again, though a little bit frightened of the strange old woman. "Now come and tell me who you are and how you came to be here," she said.

Then Gerda told her everything, and the old woman shook her head and said, "Dear me!" And when Gerda had finished her story and asked if she had seen little Kay, the woman said that he hadn't come past there; but he might, though, and Gerda mustn't be downhearted but taste some of her cherries and have a look at her flowers, which were prettier than any picture book and could each of them tell a complete story. Then she took Gerda by the hand, and they went inside the little house, and the old woman shut the door behind her.

The windows were high up on the walls, with red, blue and yellow glass in them. The daylight shone strangely into the room with all these colors, but on the table was a plate of the finest cherries, and Gerda was allowed to eat as many of them as she liked. While she was eating, the old woman combed her hair with a gold comb, and her bright yellow curls made a charming frame for the kind little face, which was so round and rosy.

"I've always longed for a nice little girl like you," said the woman. "Just you see how well we shall get on together, you and I"; and as she combed little Gerda's hair, Gerda forgot her foster brother Kay more and more. You see, the old woman could do magic, but she wasn't a wicked magician; she only did a little magic for her own enjoyment, and at present she very much wanted to keep little Gerda. So she

went out into the garden, reached out her stick to all the rose trees and, however beautifully they were in bloom, they all sank down into the black earth, leaving no sign of where they had stood. The old woman was afraid that, if Gerda saw the roses, she might think of the ones they had at home and then remember little Kay and run off.

Now she took Gerda out into the flower garden. Goodness, what fragrance and beauty there was! Every flower you could think of, at whatever season of the year, stood here in full bloom; no picture book could be more gay and attractive. Gerda jumped for joy and played about until the sun went down behind the tall cherry trees. Then she was given a charming bed with red silk pillows that were stuffed with blue violets, and there she slept and dreamt as wonderfully as any queen on her wedding day.

The next morning she was again able to play with the
flowers in the sunshine, and in this way a number of days went
by. Gerda knew every flower, but however many there were
she somehow felt there was one missing, though she didn't
know which. And then one day she was sitting looking at
the old woman's sun hat with the flowers painted on it, and
sure enough, the prettiest of them all was a rose. The woman
had forgotten to remove it from her hat that time she made
the other roses sink down into the ground. That comes of not
having your wits about you! "What!" said Gerda, "no
roses in the garden!" And she ran in and out of the flower
beds and looked and looked, but there wasn't a rose to be

found. Then she sat down and cried; but her hot tears fell just where a rose tree had sunk, and as their warmth watered the ground, the tree suddenly sprouted up, just as blooming as when it sank; and Gerda embraced it and kissed the roses, while her thoughts turned to the lovely roses at home and so to little Kay.

"Oh, how I've been delayed!" said the little girl. "I was to go and find Kay! Do you know where he is?" she asked the roses. "Do you think he's dead and gone?"

"No, he's not dead," said the roses. "You see, we've been in the earth ourselves; that's where all the dead are, but Kay wasn't there."

"Thank you," said little Gerda, and she went off to the other flowers and looked into their cups and asked, "Do you know where Kay is?"

But every flower was standing in the sun and dreaming its own fairy tale or romance. Gerda was told ever so many of those, but nobody knew anything about Kay.

And what did the tiger lily say?

"Listen to the drum—boom, boom! There are only two notes—boom, boom! Hark to the women's dirge! Hark to the cry of the priests! The Hindoo woman stands on the funeral pyre in her long red robe, the flames fly up around her and her dead husband; but the Hindoo

37

woman is thinking of the living man there in the crowd, whose eyes burn hotter than the flames, whose fiery glances come nearer to her heart than the flames that will soon burn her body to ashes. Can the heart's flame perish in the flames of the pyre?"

"I can't understand what that's all about," said little Gerda. "That's my story," said the tiger lily.

What does the convolvulus say?

"Overhanging the narrow mountain road stands an ancient castle. Creepers grow thick about the old red

walls, climbing leaf by leaf right over the balcony. And
there stands a graceful girl, leaning over the parapet and
looking down the road; no rose hangs fresher on its
spray, no apple blossom that is borne by the breeze from
its tree hovers more lightly. Listen to the frou-frou of
her splendid silk dress! 'Is he never coming?'"

"Is that Kay you mean?" asked Gerda.

"I only speak of my own story, my own dream,"
answered the convolvulus.

What does the little snowdrop say?

"Between the trees is a long board hanging by two
ropes; it's a swing. Two pretty little girls in snowy

white frocks, with long green ribbons of silk fluttering from their hats, are sitting and swinging. Their brother, who is bigger than they are, is standing up in the swing with his arm round the rope to steady himself, for in one hand he has a little bowl, in the other a clay pipe; he's blowing soap bubbles. To and fro goes the swing, and the bubbles rise floating in the air with beautiful changing colors; the last one still clings to the pipe, swaying in the wind. The swing rocks on. The little black dog, as lightly as the bubbles, rises on his hind legs, asking to be taken into the swing. It swoops past, the dog tumbles and yelps angrily, for they're teasing him; the bubbles burst. A swinging board, a picture of leaping froth—that is my song."

"I daresay that's a pretty tale, but you tell it so mournfully, and you don't say anything about Kay. What do the hyacinths say?"

"There were three beautiful sisters, with delicate skin as clear as crystal. One's dress was red, another's blue, and the third one's pure white. Hand in hand they danced beside the calm lake in the silver moonlight. They were not elf-maidens but humans. The air smelt so sweet, and the girls vanished into the wood. The air smelt still sweeter. . . . Three coffins, in which lay the beautiful sisters, glided from the heart of the wood away over the lake; fireflies flew gleaming around like little hovering tapers. Are the dancing maidens asleep or are they dead? The scent of the flowers tells that they are dead; the evening bell is tolling for the dead."

"You make me quite sad," said little Gerda. "Your scent is so strong; I can't get the dead sisters out of my mind. Oh, but is little Kay really dead? The roses have been down in the earth, and they say no."

"Ding-dong!" tolled the bells of the hyacinth. "We're not tolling for little Kay; we don't know him. We're merely singing our song, the only one we know."

And Gerda went along to the buttercup, shining out among its glistening green leaves. "How brightly you shine, little sun," said Gerda. "Tell me whether you know where I shall find my playmate."

The buttercup shone most beautifully and looked at Gerda once more. What song do you suppose the buttercup could sing? This wasn't about Kay either.

"In a small backyard God's sun was shining warmly on the first day of spring, its beams gliding down the neighbor's white walls. Nearby grew the first yellow flowers, glittering like gold in the warm rays of the sun. Old Grannie was out in her chair; her good-looking granddaughter, a humble maidservant, had come home on a short visit, and now she kissed her grandmother. There was gold, gold from the heart, in that blessed kiss. Golden lips, golden power, golden hearts in that morning hour. There! That's my little story," said the buttercup.

"My poor old Grannie!" sighed Gerda. "She's sure to be longing for me and grieving for me, as she was for little Kay. But I shall soon be home again, and then I shall bring Kay with me. . . . It's no good my asking the flowers. They only know their own songs; they can tell me nothing." And she tucked up her little frock, so as to be able to run faster. But the narcissus tapped her leg as she jumped over it. She stopped and looked at the tall yellow flower. "Perhaps you have heard something?" she asked. So she stooped right down to the narcissus. And what did she hear?

"I can see myself, I can see myself!" said the narcissus. "Dear, dear! can't you smell me? Up in the little attic room stands a little dancer. She stands, now on one leg, now on both; her high kicks are for all and sundry. Mere glamour, that's all she is. She pours out water from the teapot onto some garment she's holding; it's her stays—cleanliness is such a good thing! The white frock hanging on the peg, that's also been washed in the teapot and dried on the roof. Now she puts it on, with the saffron-yellow scarf round her neck, so that the frock gleams all the whiter. Up goes her leg! Look at her strutting on one stalk! I can see myself, I can see myself!"

"I don't care a scrap about all that," said Gerda. "It's no story for me!"—and off she ran down to the bottom of the garden.

The gate was locked, but she waggled the rusty latch till it was free; the gate flew open, and little Gerda ran out barefooted into the wide world. Three times she looked back, but nobody was following her. At last she couldn't run any more but sat down on a big stone; and when she glanced about her, she saw that the summer was over. It was late autumn, but there had been no sign of this in the beautiful garden, where there was always sunshine with flowers belonging to every season of the year.

"My, how I've dawdled!" said little Gerda. "Why, it's autumn already. I mustn't rest any longer"—and she got up to go.

Oh, how tired and sore her little feet were! The countryside looked cold and damp; the long willow leaves were quite yellow, shedding misty tears as the leaves dropped one by one. Only the sloe was still bearing fruit, so sharp as to twist your mouth all crooked. Oh, how gloomy and sad the wide world seemed!

PART FOUR

Prince and Princess

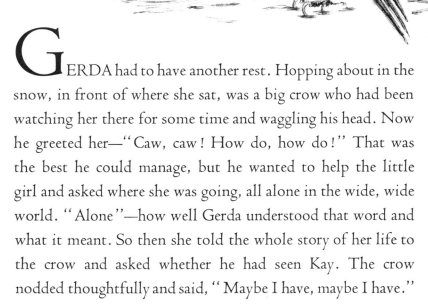

GERDA had to have another rest. Hopping about in the snow, in front of where she sat, was a big crow who had been watching her there for some time and waggling his head. Now he greeted her—"Caw, caw! How do, how do!" That was the best he could manage, but he wanted to help the little girl and asked where she was going, all alone in the wide, wide world. "Alone"—how well Gerda understood that word and what it meant. So then she told the whole story of her life to the crow and asked whether he had seen Kay. The crow nodded thoughtfully and said, "Maybe I have, maybe I have."

48

"Oh, do you think you have?" cried the little girl, nearly squeezing him to death as she kissed him.

"Now then, now then," said the crow. "I quite think it was little Kay. But by this time he will certainly have forgotten you for the Princess."

"Does he live with a princess?" asked Gerda.

"Yes, just listen," said the crow. "But I find it so difficult to talk your language. Can you understand crow language? I could tell it you better in that."

"No, I've never learnt it," said Gerda, "but Grannie can, and P language, too. I do wish I could."

"Never mind," said the crow. "I'll tell you as best I can, though it won't be up to much, I'm afraid." And then he told her what he knew.

"In the kingdom where we are now lives a Princess who is tremendously clever. You see, she has read all the newspapers there are in the world and forgotten them again. She's as clever as that. The other day she was sitting on the throne —and there's not much fun in that, so I'm told—when she happened to hum a little song that runs like this: 'Why shouldn't I have a husband?' 'Well, there's something to be said for that,' she thought. So she made up her mind to marry, but she wanted a husband who could speak up for himself when spoken to—who didn't just stand and look distinguished, for that's so very dull. Then she rang for all her court ladies, and when they heard what she meant to do, they were delighted. 'How splendid!' they all said. 'That's just what we were thinking the other day.' Believe me," added the crow, "every word I say is true. I've got a tame sweetheart who has a free run of the palace, and she has told me the whole story."

Of course, his sweetheart was also a crow, for birds of a feather flock together.

"The newspapers at once came out with a border of hearts and the Princess's monogram. You could read for yourself that any good-looking young man was free to come up to the palace and talk to the Princess; and the one who spoke so that you felt that he was quite at home there and was the best talker, he was the one the Princess meant to marry. Yes, you can take my word for it," said the crow. "It's as true as I sit here. People came in throngs. There was jostling and hustling, but every one of them failed, both on the first day and on the second. They were all good talkers out in the street, but as soon as they came to the palace and saw the guards in silver at the entrance and the lackeys in gold on the stairs and the glitter of the great lighted halls, then they became flurried; and when they stood before the throne where the Princess was sitting, they could do nothing but repeat her last remark, and she had no desire to hear that again. It was just as though people in there had been dosed with

snuff which had half sent them to sleep, until they came into
the street again; then of course they were perfect chatterboxes.
There was a long line of them stretching from the town gate
to the palace. I saw it myself," said the crow. "They soon
became hungry and thirsty, but from the palace they never received so much as a glass of tepid water. A few of the wiser
ones, it's true, had brought sandwiches with them, but they
weren't going to share them with a rival. They thought to
themselves, 'No harm in him looking hungry, then the Princess won't have him.'"

"But Kay, little Kay!" asked Gerda. "When did he
come? Was he one of all those suitors?"

"All right—give me time! We're just coming to him.
It was on the third day—up came a little chap without horse
or carriage, stepping out as bold as you please straight up to

the palace. His eyes were bright like yours, he had fine thick hair, but apart from that he was shabbily dressed."

"That was Kay!" cried Gerda. "Oh, then I've found him at last," and she clapped her hands joyfully.

"He had a little rucksack," said the crow.

"Ah, I expect that was his toboggan," said Gerda, "for he took one away with him."

"Quite possibly," said the crow. "I didn't look at it at all closely. But I know from my tame sweetheart that, when he came to the palace and saw the bodyguard in silver at the entrance and the lackeys in gold on the stairs, he wasn't in the least put out; he just gave them a nod and said how dull it must be standing on the stairs—he preferred to go inside. There the rooms were blazing with light. Privy Councillors and Ambassadors were going about in bare feet, carrying gold dishes. It was all very grand. His boots squeaked most terribly, but that didn't worry him in the slightest."

"I'm sure that must be Kay," said Gerda. "I know he had new boots on, because I heard them squeaking in Grannie's room."

"Well, they certainly did squeak!" said the crow. "And he went boldly up to the Princess, who was sitting on a pearl as big as a spinning wheel. All the ladies-in-waiting with their maids and their maids' maids, and all the gentlemen-in-waiting with their footmen and their footmen's footmen who

have pages, stood lined up all round; and the nearer they stood to the door, the haughtier they looked. The footmen's footmen's page, who always wears slippers, stands so proudly in the doorway that one can hardly bear to look at him."

"How dreadful!" said little Gerda. "And do you mean to say that Kay has won the Princess?"

"If I hadn't been a crow, I should have taken her myself, even though I'm engaged. He is said to have spoken as well as I speak, when I talk crow language, so my tame sweetheart informs me. He was bold and attractive. He hadn't in the least come to woo the Princess, but merely in order to listen to her wise conversation. He liked her, and she liked him."

"Why, of course, it was Kay," said Gerda. "He was always so clever; he could do mental arithmetic with fractions. Oh, do please take me into the palace."

"Easier said than done," said the crow. "I must talk to my tame sweetheart about it. I daresay she can advise us, for I may as well tell you that a little girl like you will never be allowed right in."

"Yes, I shall," said Gerda. "As soon as Kay hears I am there, he'll come straight out and fetch me."

"Wait for me by that stile," said the crow with a waggle of his head; and away he flew.

It was after dark before he got back. "Rah, rah!" he cawed. "I'm to give you her love, and here's a small loaf for you that she found in the kitchen; they've plenty of bread there, and you must be hungry. You can't possibly be allowed into the palace in those bare feet of yours; the guards in silver and the lackeys in gold would never let you through. But

don't cry; you shall get in all right. My sweetheart knows of a little backstair leading to the bedroom, and she knows where to find the key!''

Then they went into the garden, along the great avenue where the leaves were coming down one after another; and as one after another the lights of the palace were going out, the crow took little Gerda round to a back door that stood ajar.

Oh, how Gerda's heart went pit-a-pat with fear and longing! It was just as though she was going to do something wrong; and yet she only wanted to know if this was little Kay. Why, of course it must be him. In her mind she had a living picture of his thick hair, his intelligent eyes; and she could see plainly how he smiled, just as he used to smile when

they sat together at home among the roses. She knew how
glad he would be to see her, and to hear what a long way she
had come for his sake, and how sad they all were at home when
he never returned. Yes, she was torn between fear and joy.

Now they reached the foot of the stairs, where there was
a small lamp burning on a shelf. In the middle of the floor
stood the tame crow, turning her head this way and that to
look at Gerda, who curtsied just as Grannie had taught her.

"My betrothed has spoken so nicely of you, my dear
young lady," said the tame crow. "Your biography, as they
call it, is really most touching. If you will take the lamp, I
will lead the way. Straight ahead is our best way, so as not to
meet anyone."

"I feel as if we were being followed," said Gerda; and

something whizzed past her that looked like shadows on the wall, horses with tossing manes and scraggy legs, huntsmen, and ladies and gentlemen on horseback.

"They are dreams, that's all," said the tame crow. "They come and fetch Their Highnesses' thoughts away to hunting. That's a good thing, for now you will be able to take a longer look at them while they're asleep. But promise me that, if ever you are raised to honor and dignity, you will show a thankful heart."

"That might better have been left unsaid," said the wild crow.

By now they had got to the first room, where the walls were hung with rose-colored satin worked with flowers. Here the dreams were already whizzing past so quickly that Gerda

CONEJO ELEMENTARY SCHOOL
280 CONEJO SCHOOL ROAD
THOUSAND OAKS, CALIF. 91360

hadn't time to see if Their Highnesses were among them. Each room was more magnificent than the last; it was really quite staggering. At length they found themselves in the bedchamber.

The ceiling in here was like a great palm tree with leaves of glass, precious glass; and over the middle of the floor from a thick stem hung two beds that looked just like lilies. One of them was white; the Princess was sleeping in that one. The other was red, and it was there that Gerda was to look for little Kay. She turned back one of the red leaves and caught sight of a brown neck. It was Kay! She called out his name quite loudly, holding the lamp close to him; the dreams whirled into the room again on horseback; he woke up, turned his head and—it wasn't little Kay at all.

The Prince was like him only in the neck, but he was certainly young and handsome. Meanwhile the Princess peeped out from the white lily-bed and asked what was happening. Then little Gerda burst into tears and told her whole story, and all that the crows had done for her.

"You poor dear!" said the Prince and Princess; and they praised the two crows and told them that they weren't a bit angry with them, but they mustn't do it again. As it was, they should receive a reward. "Would you prefer to fly about on your own," asked the Princess, "or to be given a permanent place as Court Crows, with all the scraps from the kitchen?"

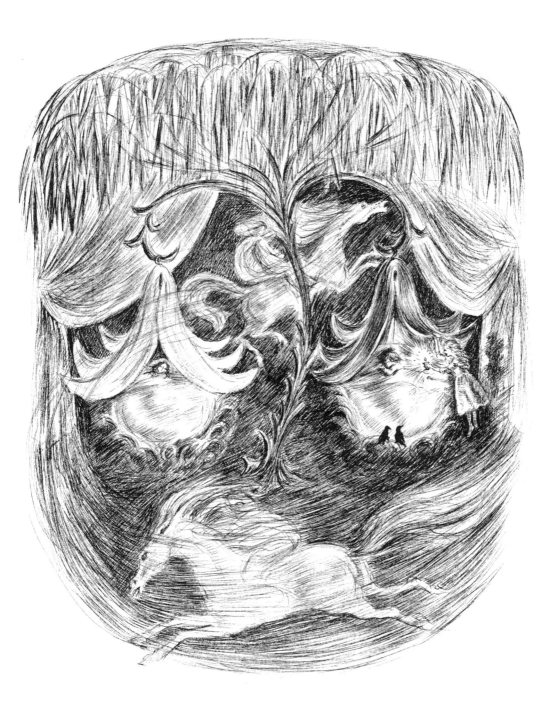

Both crows curtsied and asked for a permanency; they had an eye to the time when they would be getting on in years, and they said it was best to have something laid by "for a rainy day," as the saying is.

The Prince got up and let Gerda have his bed to sleep in; he couldn't do more than that. She folded her little hands, thinking "how kind people and birds are," then shut her eyes and went peacefully to sleep. All the dreams came flying back again, and this time they looked like angels from heaven; they were pulling a little sledge, and on it sat Kay, nodding to her. But the whole thing was only a dream, and so it vanished as soon as she woke up.

The next day she was dressed from head to foot in silk and velvet. She was invited to stay on at the palace and enjoy herself; but all she asked for was a simple horse and carriage and a pair of little boots, and she would drive out into the wide world and find Kay.

She was given both boots and muff and also the most charming clothes; and, as she was ready to leave, there at the door was a new coach of pure gold with the royal arms gleaming on its sides like a star. Coachman, footmen and outriders (for there were outriders as well) all wore gold crowns. The Prince and the Princess themselves helped her into the carriage and wished her every good fortune. The wild crow, who was

now married, went with Gerda for the first dozen miles, sitting beside her as he couldn't bear riding back to the horses. The other crow stood in the gateway flapping her wings; she didn't go with them because she suffered from headaches since getting a permanent place and too much to eat. The inside of the coach was lined with sugar twists, and the seat was stuffed with ginger nuts and jujubes.

"Good-bye! Good-bye!" cried Prince and Princess. Little Gerda wept, and the crow wept; and so they drove for some miles. Then it was the crow's turn to say good-bye; that was the saddest parting of all. He flew up into a tree and flapped his black wings as long as he could still see the coach, glittering there like the clearest sunshine.

PART FIVE

The little robber girl

As they drove through the dark forest, the coach blazed and sparkled, so that the robbers lying in wait were quite dazzled; it was more than they could bear. "It's gold, it's gold!" they screamed, dashing forward and seizing the horses. They killed the postilions, the coachman and the footmen, and dragged little Gerda out of the carriage.

"She's plump, she's appetizing, she's been fattened on

nuts," said the old robber hag, who had a long stiff beard and eyebrows that hung down over her eyes. "She's just like a little fatted lamb. Yum! Won't she taste nice!" And she pulled out her shining knife—it was terrible, the way it glittered.

"Ow!" shrieked the old hag the next instant. She had been bitten in the ear by her own little daughter who was slung on her back, as wild and mischievous as they make them. "You dirty little brat," said the mother, as she missed her chance of slaughtering Gerda.

"She shall play with me," said the little robber girl. "She shall give me her muff and her pretty frock, and she shall sleep with me in my bed." And then she gave her mother another bite, so hard that the hag went hopping round and round in her pain, and all the robbers laughed and said, "Look at her dancing with her cub!"

"I want to ride in the coach," said the little robber girl, and she had to have her own way, for she was so spoilt and wilful. So she and Gerda got in, and they drove through stubble and gorse deeper into the forest. The little robber girl was no bigger than Gerda, but sturdier, with broader shoulders and darker skin. Her eyes were quite black, with a look that was almost sad. She put her arm round little Gerda and said, "They shan't kill you unless I get angry with you. I suppose you're a princess, aren't you?"

"No," said little Gerda and told her all she had been through and how fond she was of little Kay.

The robber girl looked earnestly at her and gave a little nod as she said, "They shan't kill you, even if I do get angry with you; I shall do it myself!" And then she dried Gerda's eyes and put both her hands into the pretty muff that was so soft and warm.

Now the coach stopped. They had drawn up in the courtyard of a robbers' castle. It was full of cracks from top to bottom, ravens and crows flew out of the gaping crevices, while enormous bulldogs, each looking as if it could swallow a man, kept jumping out; but there was no barking, as that was not allowed.

A big fire was burning in the middle of the stone floor of the huge grimy old hall; the smoke trailed along under the ceiling, trying to find its way out. A great saucepan of soup was on the boil, and both hares and rabbits were turning on the spit.

"You shall sleep here tonight with me and all my pets," said the robber girl. They got something to eat and drink, and they went over to a corner where there were rugs and straw. On laths and perches above their heads nearly a hundred pigeons were roosting, apparently all asleep, but they did just stir when the two small girls came in.

"They're all mine," said the little robber girl, catching
hold of one of the nearest. She took it by the legs and shook
it till it flapped its wings. "Give her a kiss!" she cried and
flipped Gerda in the face with it. Then, pointing to a number
of bars placed in front of a hole high up in the wall, "There
are the bad lads of the forest," she went on, "behind those

bars. Those two, they'd fly away at once, if they weren't properly locked up. And here's my old sweetheart, Moo," she added, lugging out by its horns a reindeer which was tied up by means of a shiny copper ring round its neck. "He's another we have to keep a tight hold on, or he'd soon go loping off. Every blessed evening I tickle his neck for him with my sharp knife—he doesn't care for that!" And the child drew a long knife out of a crack in the wall and ran it lightly along the reindeer's neck. The poor creature let fly with its hoofs and, with a laugh, the robber girl drew Gerda down with her into bed.

"Do you always sleep with your knife beside you?" asked Gerda, looking at it rather nervously.

"Yes, I always sleep with a knife," answered the little robber girl. "You never know what may happen. But now tell me again what you told me before about little Kay and why you started out into the wide, wide world." So Gerda told her all over again, and the wood pigeons cooed up in their cage, and the other pigeons slept. The little robber girl, with one arm round Gerda's neck and the other holding the knife, went to sleep—you could hear that—but Gerda simply couldn't close her eyes; she hardly knew whether she was to live or die. The robbers sat round the fire, singing and drinking, while the old hag turned somersaults. It was a ghastly sight for the little girl.

Then the wood pigeons said, "Roo-cool! Roo-cool! we have seen little Kay. A white hen was carrying his toboggan. Kay was sitting in the Snow Queen's sledge, as it skimmed over the wood where we lay in our nest. She breathed down on us young ones, who all died except us two. Roo-cool! Roo-cool!"

"What's that you're saying up there?" Gerda called out. "Where was the Snow Queen going? Do you know anything about that?"

"She must have been making for Lapland, because they've got snow and ice up there. Ask the reindeer, who's tied up with a rope; he'll be sure to know."

"Ice and snow, yes," said the reindeer. "It's a lovely country, where you can go bounding to your heart's delight in the great glittering valleys. There the Snow Queen has her summer quarters, but her regular palace is up towards the North Pole on the island called Spitzbergen."

"Poor little Kay!" sighed Gerda.

"Well, now you must lie still," said the robber girl, "or you'll get my knife in your tummy!"

In the morning Gerda told her all that the wood pigeons had said, and the little robber girl looked quite serious; but she nodded and said, "Never mind, we can manage," and, turning to the reindeer, "Do you know where Lapland is?"

"Who should know better than I?" the animal answered with sparkling eyes. "That's where I was born and bred and first jumped about in the snowfields."

"Now listen," said the robber girl to Gerda. "You see that all our menfolk are away, but Muz is still here, and here she'll stay. Later on she'll take a pull out of that big bottle and after that have a little nap. Then I'll manage something for you." With that she jumped out of bed, gave her mother a hug round the neck and a tug of her moustache, saying, "Good morning, my own darling nanny goat!" And her mother gave her such a rap under the nose that it turned black and blue, but it was all done purely for love.

As soon as the mother had drunk from the bottle and started her forty winks, the robber girl went to the reindeer and said, "I'm just itching to tickle your neck a lot more with my sharp knife, for then you're so amusing; but never mind, I'm going to let you loose and bring you outside so that you can run off to Lapland. But you must put your best foot foremost and carry this little girl for me to the Snow Queen's palace, where her playmate is. I expect you heard what she told me, for she talked rather loud, and you're such a one for eavesdropping."

The reindeer simply jumped for joy. The robber girl lifted little Gerda onto his back and took care to strap her on tight—yes, even to give her a little cushion to sit on. "Now you're all right," she said. "You've got your fur-lined boots, for it'll be cold; but I'm keeping the muff, it's too lovely to part with. Still, we mustn't let you feel the cold. Here are my mother's big mittens that come right up to your elbows— there, in you go! Now your hands make you look just like my grubby old mother!" And Gerda wept for joy.

"I can't bear to see you blubbering," said the little robber girl. "Why, you ought to be looking extra pleased. Here's a couple of loaves and a ham, so you shan't starve." Both these were tied onto the reindeer's back. The little robber girl then opened the door, called all the big dogs in,

and slashing the rope with her knife, she said to the reindeer, "Off you go! But take care of the little girl."

Gerda held out her hands, mittens and all, to the little robber girl and said good-bye. And the reindeer flew away across stubble and scrub, through the length of the forest, over bogs and prairies, as fast as he could go. The wolves howled, the ravens squawked. "P—ff! P—ff!" kept coming from the sky; it was just as though it was sneezing red.

"They're my dear old Northern Lights," said the reindeer. "Look how they sparkle!" And then he ran on faster than ever, night and day. The loaves were eaten up, and the ham too; and at last they were in Lapland.

PART SIX

*The Lapp woman and
the Finn woman*

THEY halted at a small house, such a miserable place. The roof came right down to the ground, and the doorway was so low that the family had to crawl in and out on their stomachs. Nobody was at home except an old Lapp woman who stood frying fish over an oil lamp. The reindeer told her all about Gerda—but, first, all about himself, as he felt that was much more important, and Gerda was too done up with the cold to be able to speak.

"Oh, you poor things!" said the Lapp woman. "You've a long way to go yet. You must cover hundreds of miles before you get to the Finmark—that's where the Snow Queen has a country seat and burns Roman candles every single evening. I'll write a few words on a piece of dried cod, for I haven't got any paper, and you can take it along with you to the Finn woman up there; she can tell you better than I can what to do."

By this time Gerda had warmed up and had something to eat and drink, so the Lapp woman wrote a few words on a piece of dried cod and told Gerda to mind and take care of it. Then she strapped her tight again onto the reindeer and off they went. "P—ff! P—ff!" they heard spluttering in the sky, and all night long they saw the loveliest blue Northern Lights burning. At last they reached the Finmark and knocked on the Finn woman's chimney, for she hadn't even a door.

Inside, the air was so hot that the Finn woman herself went about with hardly a stitch of clothing. She was dumpy and dark-skinned. She at once loosened little Gerda's clothes and took off her mittens and boots, otherwise she would have been much too warm; she also put a lump of ice on the reindeer's head, and after that she read what was written on the dried cod. She read it over three times, till she knew it by heart, and then she popped the fish into the stock pot, for it was quite eatable and she never wasted anything.

First, the reindeer told his own story, and then little Gerda's; and the Finn woman's knowing eyes twinkled, but she didn't say a word.

"You're so clever," said the reindeer. "I know you can tie up all the winds in the world with a thread of cotton. If the skipper undoes one knot, he gets a good wind; if he undoes a second, it blows hard; and when he undoes the third and the fourth, there's a gale that sends the trees of the forest crashing. Will you give this little girl a drink that will lend her the strength of twelve men so that she can get the better of the Snow Queen?"

"The strength of twelve men?" said the Finn woman; "I'm afraid that wouldn't go far!" Then she went over to a shelf and took down a big rolled-up parchment, which she unrolled. There was strange writing on it, and the Finn woman stood reading it till the sweat poured from her forehead.

But the reindeer pleaded again so hard for little Gerda, and Gerda looked with such tearful beseeching eyes at the Finn woman that the twinkle came back into hers, and drawing the reindeer into a corner, she put a fresh lump of ice on his head and had a whispered conversation with him.

"Yes, it's quite true, little Kay is with the Snow Queen and finds everything to his liking and thinks it's the nicest place in the world; but that's only because he's got a glass splinter in his heart and a tiny fragment in his eye. These must come out first, or else he'll never be human again, and the Snow Queen will keep her power over him."

79

"Well, but isn't there some physic little Gerda can take that will give her power over everything?"

"I can't give her greater power than she has already. Don't you see how great that is? Don't you see how man and beast feel obliged to serve her, and how far she has come in the world in her bare feet? She mustn't learn of her power from us; it lies in her heart, in her being a dear innocent child. If she can't by herself reach the Snow Queen and get rid of the glass from little Kay, then there's nothing we can do to help. The Snow Queen's garden begins about ten miles further on. You can carry the little girl so far, then set her down close to the large bush with red berries that's standing there in the snow. Don't stay gossiping, but make haste back here." Then the Finn woman lifted little Gerda onto the back of the reindeer, who dashed off as fast as he could.

"Oh, I've forgotten my boots! I've forgotten my mittens!" little Gerda called out, directly she felt the piercing cold. But the reindeer didn't dare stop; he ran on till he came to the large bush with the red berries. There he put Gerda down and kissed her on the mouth; big shining tears ran down the animal's cheeks, and then back he dashed once more as fast as he could go. There was poor Gerda, left standing without shoes, without gloves, in the middle of the terrible icy Finmark.

She started running forward as well as she could, but then a whole regiment of snowflakes appeared. They didn't fall from the sky, for that was quite clear and glittering with Northern Lights. The snowflakes came running along the

ground, and the nearer they came, the bigger they grew. Gerda remembered no doubt how big and curious they had looked that time she saw them through the burning-glass; but these were altogether bigger and more terrifying—they were alive, they were the Snow Queen's advance guards, they had the most fantastic shapes. Some of them looked like vicious great hedgehogs, others like a lot of knotted snakes sticking out their heads, and others like fat little bears with bristling

pelts; all of them were glittering white, all of them living snowflakes.

Then little Gerda said the Lord's Prayer, and the cold was so intense that she could see her own breath coming just like smoke out of her mouth; it grew thicker and thicker, until it took the shape of little shining angels who got bigger and bigger as they touched the ground. They all had helmets on their heads and spears and shields in their hands. Their

numbers grew and grew and, by the time Gerda had finished
her prayer, there was a whole legion of them around her. They
struck with their spears at the horrible snowflakes, so that
they flew into a hundred pieces, and little Gerda could walk
on without fear or danger. The angels patted her feet and
hands for her, so that she didn't feel the cold so much and was
able to walk briskly on towards the Snow Queen's palace. . . .

But now it's time for us to see how Kay is getting on.
It's quite certain he hasn't given a thought to Gerda; least of
all does he imagine that she's standing outside the palace.

PART SEVEN

*What happened at
the Snow Queen's palace
and afterwards*

THE walls of the palace were built of drifting snow,
and the windows and doors of cutting winds. There were over
a hundred rooms, just as the blizzards had made them, the
largest stretching out for miles, all of them lit up by the vivid
Northern Lights: huge, empty, ice-cold and glittering. Never

was there any jollification, not even so much as a little dance for the bears, when the gale could play the horn and the polar bears get up on their hind legs and show off their party manners. Never a little social with mouth-slapping and paw-rapping; never the smallest tea-fight for the snowy young vixens; all was bare, bleak and vast in the halls of the Snow Queen. The Northern Lights flared up each time so punctually that you could work out just when they would be at their highest point and when at their lowest. In the middle of the empty unending snow hall lay a frozen lake. It was cracked into a thousand pieces, but each piece looked so exactly like the other that it was quite a work of art. It was here, in the middle, that the Snow Queen would sit, when she was at home; she would say that she was sitting at the Glass of Reason, and that was the one and only glass in the world.

Little Kay was quite blue with cold—in fact, almost black. But he never noticed it, because the Snow Queen had kissed the cold shivers out of him, and his heart was little more than a lump of ice. He was engaged in dragging along some sharp-edged flat pieces of ice, which he was trying in all sorts of positions; he wanted to make some kind of pattern from them, in the same way as we arrange little wooden pieces when we do a jigsaw puzzle. Kay, too, was busy with patterns, most complicated ones; it was the Great Mental Ice Puzzle. To him these patterns seemed most remarkable and highly important; that was the result of the glass splinter in his eye. He put together whole patterns which made up a written word, but he never could manage the one word he was after—the word ETERNITY. And yet the Snow Queen had said to him, "If you can find me that pattern, then you shall be your own

88

master, and I'll make you a present of the whole world and a pair of new skates.'' But he just couldn't.

''Now I must tear off to the warm countries,'' said the Snow Queen. ''I want to go and peep into the black pots.'' She meant the burning mountains that we call Etna and Vesuvius. ''I shall whiten them a little—one generally has to ; it does them good after all the lemons and grapes.'' So the Snow Queen flew off, and Kay was left looking at the pieces of ice and thinking, thinking, until he was quite dizzy. There he sat, quite still, without moving a muscle ; you might have thought he was frozen to death.

It was at this moment that Gerda walked into the palace through the great gate of cutting winds. But she said an evening prayer, and the winds died down as if they were sleepy, and she stepped into the great empty shivery halls—there was Kay! She knew him at once, rushed and flung her arms round his neck and held him tight, exclaiming, "Kay, dear, darling Kay! I've found you at last!"

But he sat there quite still, all cold and stiff.... Then little Gerda wept hot tears—they fell on his breast, they forced their way into his heart, they thawed out the lump of ice and dissolved the little bit of glass that was there. He looked at her, and she sang the words of the hymn:

The valley glows with many a rose,
and there we meet the Sacred Child.

Then Kay burst into tears. He cried so much that the splinter of glass trickled out of his eye; he recognized her and shouted joyfully, "Gerda, dear, darling Gerda! Where ever have you been all this time? And where have I been?" Then he looked about him. "How cold it is! How empty and huge!" And he kept tight hold of Gerda, while she laughed and cried for joy. They were so happy that even the flat pieces of ice danced

with delight, and when they got tired and calmed down, there they were forming the very word that the Snow Queen had said Kay must find out, then he should be his own master and she would give him the whole world and a pair of new skates.

And Gerda kissed his cheeks, and they bloomed once more. She kissed his eyes, and they sparkled like hers. She kissed his hands and feet, and he was well and strong again. Let the Snow Queen come home now if she liked—there was his release, written out in glittering ice.

Then hand in hand they wandered out of the vast palace, talking about Grannie and the roses up on the roof. Wherever they went, the winds died down and the sun broke through; and when they got to the bush with the red berries, there was the reindeer waiting for them. He had a young doe with him; her udders were full of warm milk for the two children, and she kissed them on the mouth. They took Kay and Gerda on their backs and carried them, first to the Finn woman, where they warmed themselves in her hot room and were told about the way home, and after that to the Lapp woman, who had made some new clothes for them and put her sledge in repair.

The reindeer and the young doe bounded alongside and kept with them as far as the frontier, where the first green shoots were beginning to peep out. There Kay and Gerda parted from the reindeer and the Lapp woman, and they all said good-bye to each other. And now the first little birds were beginning to twitter, the first green buds to appear in the forest; and out of it came a young girl riding a magnificent horse, which Gerda remembered seeing harnessed to the gold coach. The young girl had a bright red cap on her head and pistols at her belt. It was the little robber girl, who was tired of being at home and was now making for the north; but if she didn't like it there, she was going to try somewhere else. She recognized Gerda immediately, and Gerda recognized her; they were overjoyed.

"You're a queer sort of globe-trotter!" she said to little Kay. "I wonder if you're worth running after to the ends of the earth."

But Gerda patted her cheek and asked after the Prince and Princess.

"They've gone abroad," said the robber girl.

"Well, but what about the crow?" asked Gerda. "Ah, the crow's dead," she answered. "The tame sweetheart's a widow now and goes about with a bit of black wool round her leg. She's terribly sorry for herself, but it's all put on. Well, now tell me about yourself and how you managed to get hold of Kay."

Then Gerda and Kay between them told her the whole story. "And snip, snap, snout, your tale is out!" said the robber girl. She shook hands with them both and promised that, if ever she passed through their town, she would come up and pay them a call; and then away she rode into the wide world.

But Kay and Gerda walked on hand in hand, and as they went, spring came to meet them in all its beauty of blossom and greenery. The church bells rang out, and they recognized the tall steeples and the large town—it was the very one they lived in. And they went into the town, straight along to their grandmother's door, up the stairs, and into the room, where everything was just as they left it and the clock said, "tick,

94

tick," and the hands were still going round. But as they went through the door they noticed they were now grown up. The roses in the boxes over the gutter were beginning to flower at the open windows, and their own little stools were still in their place. So Kay and Gerda sat down and took each other by the hand. The cold empty splendor of the Snow Queen's palace was now forgotten like a bad dream. Grannie was sitting there in God's clear sunshine, reading aloud from the Bible, "Except ye become as little children, ye shall not enter into the Kingdom of Heaven."

Kay and Gerda looked into each other's eyes, and all at once they understood the meaning of the old hymn:

> The valley glows with many a rose,
> and there we meet the Sacred Child.

There they sat, the two of them, grown up and yet children—children at heart. And it was summertime, warm delicious summertime.

Mw